Tim Winton was born in Perth in 1960. He grew up on the coast of Western Australia where he became a keen diver, angler and beachcomber. Winton's stories began to be published in Australian newspapers and magazines while he was still a teenager and he has been a professional writer for fifteen years.

In 1981 his first novel won the *Australian*/Vogel Award and his other prizes include the Banjo, the Wilderness Society Environment Award and the Miles Franklin (twice). In 1995 he was shortlisted for the Booker Prize. His fiction is published in ten languages and has been adapted for stage, screen and radio. He lives with his wife and three children in Western Australia.

Other books by Tim Winton

NOVELS
An Open Swimmer
Shallows
That Eye, The Sky
In the Winter Dark
Cloudstreet
The Riders
Dirt Music
The Turning

STORIES
Scission
Minimum of Two

FOR YOUNGER READERS
Jesse
Lockie Leonard, Human Torpedo
The Bugalugs Bum Thief
Lockie Leonard, Scumbuster
Lockie Leonard, Legend
Blueback
The Deep

NON-FICTION
Land's Edge
*Down to Earth (*with Richard Woldendorp*)*

TIM
WINTON
BLUEBACK

PICADOR
Pan Macmillan Australia

First published 1997 by Pan Macmillan Australia Pty Limited
This Picador edition published 1999 by Pan Macmillan Australia Pty Limited
St Martins Tower, 31 Market Street, Sydney

Reprinted 2004, 2005

Text: Copyright © Tim Winton 1997
Illustrations: Copyright © Andrew Davidson 1998

National Library of Australia
cataloguing-in-publication data:

Winton, Tim, 1960- .

Blueback.

ISBN 0 330 36162 7.

I. Title.

A823.3

'Portrait of Luke' from *A Counterfeit Silence* by Randolph Stow
Copyright © Randolph Stow
Reprinted by permission of Angus & Robertson Publishers.

'Carmel Point' from *Selected Poems* by Robinson Jeffers.
Copyright © 1994 by Robinson Jeffers.
Reprinted by permission of Random House, Inc.

Printed in Australia by McPherson's Printing Group

for

Jesse, Harry and Alice

who love the sea

... for today, for a while, his eyes are open harbours

and the dolphins of his thoughts cannot obscure

(look down) the coral bones of all our ancestors.

Randolph Stow, *Portrait of Luke*

... As for us:

We must uncenter our minds from ourselves;

We must unhumanize our views a little,

and become confident

As the rock and ocean that we were made from.

Robinson Jeffers, *Carmel Point*

Chapter One

Just as the sun came up, Abel pulled on his wetsuit and ran down the jetty. Already his mother was in the dinghy with the outboard motor running. It was cold this morning and Abel was still half asleep. He got down into the boat, untied the bowline and pushed them clear. With a purr of the outboard they surged away.

In the bow, he looked around, slowly waking up in the cold rush of air. Sunlight caught the windows of the shack above the beach so that every pane of glass looked like a little fire. He watched his mother's hair blow back off her shoulders. She squinted a little. Her skin was tanned and wrinkled from the sun. He felt the sea pulsing under him as the little boat skimmed across the bay.

'Good morning, sleepyhead,' said his mother. 'Better get your gear out.'

He bent down to the plastic dive crate and pulled out his fins, snorkel and mask. He found his weightbelt and bag and screwdriver and laid them on the seat beside him.

After a while his mother steered them around the front of Robbers Head and cut the motor. The anchor went down into the dark, clear water and everything was quiet.

'Stay close today, okay?'

'Okay,' he said, pulling on his fins and rubbing spit into his mask so it wouldn't fog up under water.

His mother pitched over the side, her fins flashing upwards. The boat rocked a little and Abel pulled his mask on and followed her.

He fell back into the water with a cold crash. A cloud of bubbles swirled around him, clinging to his skin like pearls. Then he cleared his snorkel — phhht! — and rolled over to look down on the world underwater.

Great, round boulders and dark cracks loomed below. Tiny silver fish hung in nervous schools. Seaweed trembled in the gentle current. Orange starfish and yellow plates of coral glowed from the deepest slopes where his mother was already gliding like a bird.

Abel loved being underwater. He was ten years old and could never remember a time when he could not dive. His mother said he was a diver before he was born; he floated and swam in the warm ocean inside her for nine months, so maybe it came naturally. He liked to watch his mother cruise down into the deep in her patchy wetsuit. She looked like a scarred old seal in that thing. She was a beautiful swimmer, relaxed and strong. Everything he knew on land or under the sea he learnt from her.

With a quick breath he followed her down. He clutched his bag and screwdriver and felt the pressure prick his ears. On the bottom his mother had found what they came for. Abalone. In a seam along the smooth granite rock, the shellfish grew round and silver like shiny hubcaps. They clamped tight to the rock and only a hefty screwdriver could budge them.

Abel saw the flash of his mother's screw-driver. She prised an abalone off the rock and a little puff of sediment rose around her. The muscle twitched in its shell. The meat was white with a green lip. His mother shoved it into her bag and moved along to pick out another.

Abel ran out of breath. He kicked back to the shining surface and hung there panting fresh air for a moment. His mother came gliding up with three abalone in her bag already. Her snorkel whooshed beside him. In a moment they dived again to work along the bottom, picking abalone and filling their bags. Up and down they went, hanging onto each breath, taking a couple of abalone from each clump, leaving the rest to breed and grow. Small fish came out of the weed and crevices to snaffle bits of meat and pick over the sediment they stirred up. Wrasse, sweep, scalyfins, blennies, foxfish and blue devils — all kinds of reef fish — darted about them in bursts of colour.

On the deepest dive, at his limit, Abel was almost at the end of his breath when he felt a rush in the water behind him. It felt like something big, like his mother passing. But out the corner of his eye he saw a blue shadow that blocked out the sun. He whirled around to see a huge mouth and an eye the size of a golfball coming at him. The mouth opened. He saw massive pegs of teeth as it came on in a terrible rush. Abel screamed in his snorkel and pushed hard off the bottom but the big blue shadow suddenly had him by the hand. The abalone he was holding came tearing out of his fingers. Abel thought he was about to die. He felt pain shoot up his arm. A vast flat tail blurred across his body. And then it was gone.

Abel shot to the surface and burst into the fresh air with a shriek. He wheeled around, looking for danger, waiting for another rush from the lurking shadow. His whole body quaked and trembled. He looked at his hand; a tiny thread of blood curled into the water. It was only a scratch.

His mother came slowly upward with her bag full. She gave him the thumbs up.

'Get in the boat!' he shouted when she surfaced. 'There's something down there!'

She grabbed him by the arm and squeezed. 'It's okay, love.'

'Mum, it nearly got me!'

'Close call, eh?' she said with a smile.

'Look, it took skin off my fingers!'

'Look down now.'

'Let's get to the boat. Please!'

'Just look down,' said his mother.

Reluctantly he stuck the snorkel back in his mouth and put his head under. Near the bottom, in the mist left from their abalone gathering, a huge blue shadow twitched and quivered. There it was, not a shark, but the biggest fish he had ever seen. It was gigantic. It had fins like ping pong paddles. Its tail was a blue-green rudder. It looked as big as a horse.

'Come down,' said his mother. 'Let's look at him.'

'I — I thought it was a shark.'

'He sure took you by surprise,' she said, laughing. 'That's a blue groper. Biggest I've ever seen.'

Abel and his mother slid down into the deep again and saw the fish hovering then turning, eyeing them cautiously as they came. It twitched a little and edged along in front of them to keep its distance. The big gills fanned. All its armoured scales rippled in lines of green and black blending into the dizziest blue. The groper moved without the slightest effort. It was magnificent; the most beautiful thing Abel had ever seen.

After a few moments his mother eased forward with an abalone in one outstretched hand. The groper watched her. It turned away for a moment, afraid, and then came round in a circle. Abel couldn't hold his breath much longer but he didn't want to miss anything so he hung there above his mother and the fish with his lungs nearly bursting.

The groper arched back. The mosaic of its

scales shone in the morning sun. His mother got close enough to touch the fish with the meat of the abalone. The fish trembled in the water and then froze for a moment as though getting ready to flee. She ran the shellmeat along its fat bottom lip and let go. The fish powered forward, chomped the abalone and hurtled off into a dark, deep hole.

*

The pair of them climbed into the boat laughing. They piled their catch into the crate and pressed towels against their glowing faces.

'I can't believe it,' said Abel. 'It's big enough to eat your arm off.'

'He must be old to grow that big,' said his mother as she pulled on the starter rope.

'He's so blue.'

'And smart,' she said. 'He knew what he

was doing. We're lucky, you know, lucky to see such a thing.'

They skimmed back around into the bay across the slick green water toward the jetty and the shack that was their home.

Abel Jackson had lived by the sea here at Longboat Bay ever since he could remember. His whole life was the sea and the bush. Every day was special, his mother always told him this, but it all became much more precious the day he first shook hands with old Blueback.

Chapter Two

Even while Abel helped his mother shell
the abalone and trim the meat for freezing
that first day, he was already planning to
get back out to Robbers Head to see the
groper again. His mother set up a drum of
seawater on a gas flame to boil the empty
shells clean. People in town bought the shells
as souvenirs. It made them a few dollars. As

Abel carried the abalone meat up to the freezer shed an idea came to him. He'd call the fish 'Blueback'. He didn't know why but it seemed right. He had never seen anything so blue in all his life, not the sky nor the sea. Blueback. Yes.

'Will it be there again tomorrow?' he asked at breakfast.

'Gropers are territorial,' said his mother dishing up the eggs. 'That means they stay in the same area most of their life.'

'Can we go tomorrow?'

'There's school tomorrow. Besides, we have enough abalone now.'

'We could fish off Robbers Head. There's jewfish out there.'

'After school, then. If the weather holds.'

*

After breakfast Abel carried seaweed up to the fruit trees. He filled bags of washed kelp and heaved them up the slope from the jetty to the orchard. The ground up there really stank. Every year Abel and his mother netted pilchards and salmon to dig into the sand for fertiliser. The whole bay would stink for a week as they chopped the fish into the rich compost they made from tree bark, vegetable scraps and seagrass.

Abel laid the kelp around the fig trees and the apricots. There were orange and lemon trees in the orchard as well as olives and mulberries. Every row of trees jangled with bells to keep away the birds. After emptying each bag, Abel looked out over Longboat Bay and thought about seeing Blueback again.

Abel and his mother lived off the sea and the land. Jacksons had been living here like this for more than a hundred years. The land at Longboat Bay had been theirs since whaling times and all the land around them was national park. Behind the orchard, where the bushland and forest began, there was a little family cemetery, a patch of white crosses and headstones to mark all the Jacksons who had lived and died here. There was a cross there for Abel's father but no body was ever buried beneath it. On their own now, Abel and his mother fished and grew fruit and vegetables. They kept ducks and chooks for meat and eggs and had a goat or two for milk. There was no mains electricity out at Longboat Bay, no water except rainwater and no TV. It was hard work sometimes, living the way they did, but Abel had never known any other life. He roamed in the forest of the national park and swam in the sea every day. He was lonely sometimes but he liked being with his mother.

Some nights he stood on the back verandah to watch the kangaroos gather in the orchard. They came in large groups to graze in the open. Looking at those roos he wondered what it would be like to live in a big family like one of theirs. He figured it would be crowded and noisy but probably a lot of fun as well. When I'm older, he thought, I'll have a family of my own. I'll make sure we're a crowd, a real mob.

When Abel got back to the house he could hear his mother clanking around in the shed. She was working on the diesel generator with grease all up her arms. His mother was a good mechanic. She kept the truck and the outboard going on her own. She said every engine was just a puzzle to solve.

'Mum?'

'Yep.'

'Let's not wait till tomorrow.'

'For what?'

'To see Blueback. The groper.'

'Blueback, is he? I must say, you're keen, love.'

'It's Sunday. We could go back out to Robbers Head after lunch.'

His mother thought about it for a moment. 'Okay, why not. If the weather holds.'

'Oh, yes!'

*

After lunch Abel and his mother anchored the dinghy off Robbers Head and dived into the luminous water. Brilliant red schools of nannygai parted before them as they slipped down. They found the patch of abalone but Blueback was nowhere to be seen. Above them, on the rippling shiny surface, the boat hung like a kite; it tugged on its anchor rope and turned to and fro.

Abel's mother swam from one rock crevice to the next, looking for the big blue groper, but couldn't find him anywhere. Abel glided along behind her, following her gaze. In a dim cleft they came upon a big, twitching crayfish. Abel's mother reached in and dragged it bucking and flapping out of the cave and both of them kicked up toward the surface. Quite suddenly, Blueback was above them. He swooped down and took the bucking cray in a single swipe and was gone in a flick of the tail.

'Well, he's a crafty old thing, I'll give him that,' said Abel's mother as they floated, puffing and blowing, on the surface. 'I was looking forward to a crayfish dinner.'

'Let's go back down,' said Abel, still tingling with excitement.

So they dived again but Blueback was holed up somewhere scoffing crayfish and wouldn't come out. In the end the water got cold. They headed home.

Chapter Three

Abel caught the bus into school next morning. He kept Blueback to himself, a secret from the rest of the world. The schoolbus rattled along the Longboat Bay road, spitting gravel and raising dust until it reached the highway.

'Gettin' any fish out there?' called Merv the driver.

'A few,' said Abel.

Merv laughed. 'You Jacksons have been sayin' that for a century. Ha, ha, a few. You always get a few.'

They picked up kids from farms along the highway and the school day began.

All day Abel daydreamed about Blueback. He wondered how old that fish must be to have grown to such a size. Just imagine all the things he'd seen! All the creatures that had come and gone around him all those years, the boats and people and time that had passed out there at Robbers Head. Even the reef would have changed in that time.

Abel knew that if you cut down a karri tree you could see its age by the growth rings in the timber. You could even tell the changes in seasons, see the droughts and the good years written into its heart. People spoke to each other. They told stories and remembered. But a fish was different. All its years were secret, a mystery. He wondered if a fish even remembered. When a fish died, did all those years just vanish? Abel thought about it for hours. He got into trouble with the teacher for daydreaming again. He was given a hundred lines:

> *I must not daydream in class*
> *I must not daydream in class*
> *I must not*

But after fifty lines or so he went back to thinking about Blueback and never actually finished. The teacher sent him home with a hundred more.

After school Abel collected the eggs and changed the ducks' water. The ducks swam in an old pink bathtub. Their water went greeny-black after a few days and stank to high heaven. Bailing it out was a messy job but he liked to hose the ducks down after the bath was refilled. They stood with their chests out as he drilled them with hosewater. They looked like silly fat businessmen in white suits. They shook their heads like bankers.

When his mother finished fuelling up the generator they climbed into their wetsuits and headed out to see Blueback.

The old fish scooted in circles as they dived into the clear deep. It was almost as though he was waiting for them. He came in close as they reached the bottom. Abel stretched out and touched him under the chin. Blueback's eyes rolled, watching him. His fins vibrated. Abel felt the enormous weight of the fish's body as it brushed him. His mother floated nearby, her hair like kelp above her.

Up and down they dived, stretching every lungful of air, while Blueback hovered around, checking them out. In the end, Abel found he could hold out a hand to Blueback's big blunt snout while the fish pushed him backwards through the water. It was nerve-wracking at first because Blueback was strong enough to crush him against the reef or even grab his arm and drag him over the dark drop-off where the water went all hazy, deep as deep. But the boy and the fish fooled about safely in silence, back and forward, familiar as old friends.

Abel rode home in the boat with his head buzzing.

✻

By the open fire Abel did his homework. One day, he decided, I'll study fish until I know what they think. I'll become an expert.

He looked up at the mantelpiece and the old photo of his father. Abel didn't really remember him. He died when Abel was two years old but the bay and the garden and the house were like a memory of him. Abel saw his mother as a memory of him. Everything she did seemed to have something of his father about it — the way she was with boats and motors, her tough working hands.

Abel knew she remembered his father every day. Near the orchard there was an old peppermint tree with a deep fork in it. His mother kept a candle there and some pearl shells and a dolphin he once carved from driftwood. Some days she stayed up at that tree for hours. Crying sometimes, thinking, remembering.

Abel's father had been a pearl diver. Every year he went north for the pearling season. He came back with the year's money and swore he would never go back. It was boring work, he said. But he always went back. And then one year a tiger shark took him. The crew of the lugger pulled in his air hose to find no one at the end of it. They found his fins on the murky bottom of Roebuck Bay but his body was never recovered.

As well as wondering what fish thought, Abel also wondered what dead people thought. Both things were mysteries; they tied his mind up in knots but he never gave up wondering.

Chapter Four

Every day he could, Abel swam with Blue-back at Robbers Head. Some days the fish didn't show. Other days he was nervy and distant, but often he was simply bold, even mischievous. Abel kept him a secret but as spring became summer it wasn't safe to keep it to himself.

Every year boats came into Longboat Bay

on their way around the coast. They were a long way from any harbour. Yachts pulled in to shelter from bad weather, sometimes, but mostly their visitors were tuna boats and sharkfishermen who anchored for a rest overnight and came ashore to say hello and trade supplies. Some skippers let their crews snorkel off the boats to spear fish or catch crays. And every year Mad Macka the abalone diver worked his licensed patch around the coast. Sooner or later someone was bound to run into Blueback and that someone might be quick enough to spear him. Groper were good food; they fetched a big price at the market. The old fish was wily, but a good spearfisher might put a shaft through him if he was patient.

So that season, as boats came and went, Abel's mother told each skipper that there was a big blue off Robbers Head, a monster fish they should leave alone. Fishing people respected Dora Jackson. They talked about her with a kind of awe. They took notice of what she said. When she told Mad Macka he smiled and said he knew all about it. They needn't worry, he said, old Blueback was safe with him.

'That fish!' said Macka. 'Cheekiest fish I ever saw. Steals everything. Eat the wetsuit offa ya if ya stayed still long enough.'

So Blueback stayed on at Robbers Head without being hassled. Skippers talked about him now and then and stories grew about the kid and the fish. Abel took sailors and deckhands out to see him. He figured his secret was safer out in the open but he wondered if one day Blueback might be so well known that some deadhead would come out there just to kill him and make themselves famous for five minutes. Abel knew all about fishing for food but he couldn't understand people who wanted photos of themselves beside huge dead fish, fish killed for fun. One season grew into another and Abel grew old enough to take the dinghy out on his own. He swam with Blueback whenever work and the weather permitted. Some days he collected rock crabs on shore and fed them to the gluttonous old fish. Crabs were clearly his favourite. Just the hint of crab in the water sent Blueback into a darting, shivering frenzy.

Some afternoons Abel sat on the jetty to watch Macka work his way across the bay. His yellow boat throbbed with the sound of the air compressor. From the compressor the orange hose coiling out into the water took air down to the seabed where Macka worked out of sight, pulling abalone, taking a few from each seam, leaving plenty behind for next year.

'It's not safe out there alone,' said Abel's mother. 'Not like that, using a hookah on your own with all that abalone meat in the water. He should have an offsider. He's crazy.'

'Guess that's why they call him Mad Macka,' said Abel.

It was a lonely sight, that was for sure. An empty boat drifting, tugged along by an invisible diver at the end of an airhose. Nothing moving on deck except that flapping blue and white diver's flag. A few years ago an abalone diver had been bitten in half by a great white shark further along the coast. Divers usually worked in pairs for safety. But Macka didn't want an offsider; he liked it on his own. Every season Macka came, Dora

Jackson made the diver welcome in the bay, but Abel often saw his mother shudder apprehensively at the sight of that lonely yellow boat on the bay.

*

One season, the year Abel turned twelve, he came out of the vegetable garden with an armful of sweetcorn and, looking out across the bay, he realised that Macka's boat was silent. It had been thrumming all morning and now it hung there quiet on the still sea. The orange hose was out, Macka was underwater but the compressor had stopped. Abel knew it meant something terrible. He dropped his bundle of corn.

'Mum!'

The pair of them raced to their dinghy and tore across the bay. They tied up alongside the abalone boat. Abel's mother stripped off her jeans and jumped aboard. She snatched up Macka's speargun and opened his toolbox.

Abel watched anxiously as she fitted a power head to the spear. Her hands shook a little.

'Toss me my fins and mask,' she said.

Abel threw them across. Macka's boat was eerie. The only sound was the crackle and flap of the flag.

'He's out of fuel,' said his mother.

That could only mean two or three things and none of them meant Macka would be coming up alive. Abel looked at the power-head his mother screwed onto the spear. One of those could blow a hole in the side of a boat. But could it stop a great white?

'Stay in the boat,' said his mother. 'Do *not* get in the water, Abel.'

She plunged into the water and Abel watched her follow Macka's airhose down into the steely deep. Her red fins flashed like a siren light. Abel's heart beat so hard it hurt. He'd never seen someone dead before. Oh God, he thought, don't let a shark take *her* too. Abel couldn't imagine life without his mother.

A few seconds later Dora Jackson spouted beside the boat. She unscrewed the powerhead and passed the speargun up. She pulled off her fins and climbed the ladder into Macka's boat.

'Was it a shark?'

His mother began to pull on the hose. 'No. There isn't a mark on him. I think he's had a heart attack. Maybe he just couldn't swim back to the surface. Poor man probably just lay on the bottom helpless until his compressor ran out of fuel. Get a grapple, love.'

'So he's dead?'

She heaved on the hose and it coiled behind her. 'Yeah, mate. He's drowned. He's gone.'

Abel jumped across and helped her haul poor Macka in. A cloud of gulls hung over the two boats. The sky was wide and blue above them and the bay was quiet, so quiet.

Chapter Five

The year he turned thirteen Abel Jackson went away to school. Longboat Bay was a long way from towns big enough for their own high school so he had to live in a hostel in a big town inland.

On his last day home he planned to swim with Blueback. He wanted to find a few juicy crabs and feed the old fish and fool around with him a good long while. But the sea was up, huge, jagged swells thundered against the coast, and it was impossible to go out on the bay. So he spent his last morning chopping wood glumly for his mother. He split karri blocks for two hours and stacked them in the woodshed. When he was finished he walked up through the grapevines and the orchard and into the national park that surrounded the bay.

Birds chattered and flashed from tree to tree. The ground was heavy with bark and leaf litter. High above him the wind groused in the crowns of the karris. The flaky trunks swallowed him up like a noisy mob. From high on the ridge he looked down at the bay. Out at Robbers Head the sea heaved itself at the cliffs. Towers of white-water lifted in the air. Inside the bay was a rash of foamy whitecaps and wind-streaks. Waves smashed against the jetty. The dinghy was hauled up on the beach and Macka's abalone boat still stood neglected on its trailer.

At the house he saw the flap of poultry, splashes of colour on the washing line and smoke angling from the house chimney. His whole life lay down there; everything he knew. He didn't want to leave it but there was no way around the fact — he had to go. He'd just have to count the weeks till the holidays.

On his way back down, Abel stopped at the peppermint tree his mother used as a kind of shrine to his father. The tree was stout and sinewy and its thin leaves were fragrant. He reached into his pocket and pulled out a piece of craggy white coral. He laid it in the tree fork with all the other bits and pieces, pressed his cheek against the rough bark of the trunk and went down to where his mother was beginning to pack the truck.

*

I'll wither up and die away from this place, he thought as they bumped off down the gravel road. This is my place. This is where I belong.

*

Abel didn't wither and die but he didn't care much for the big town he moved to. It was a long way inland and surrounded by wheat as far as the eye could see. The land was flat. All the trees were long gone, bulldozed and burnt to make way for croplands, and nothing seemed to move out there now except the endless paddocks of wheat-ears. Abel felt hemmed in. Everyone bunched up together in town as though they felt it too. Abel never seemed to be alone. He went to school in a crowd and he came back to the hostel in a crowd. Everywhere he went there were doors slamming and shoes clacking and a competing roar of voices. Even in his bed at night his dormitory was full of coughs and cries and the clanking of pipes.

Abel felt surrounded. He did his best to cope. He worked hard at school and made friends. New things and fresh faces came his way but here, where everyone seemed to move faster and bustle along, time passed more slowly than it ever did back at Longboat Bay. Home throbbed in him like a headache.

Only in his sleep did Abel feel free. In his dreams Blueback loomed up at him out of the blurry dark. The old fish's eye was like a turning moon. In his sleep Abel swam and remembered and saw things he needed, things he wanted to see, and some things he didn't expect.

Once in his dreams, Abel swam with Blueback down into a deep crevice where the water was cold and lit palest blue. He held onto the fish's fins and let himself be taken. At the bottom of the rock shaft was a great gathering. Abel saw men in uniform, dead sailors floating in the current. Their eyes were open and their brass buttons gleamed. They hung there like starfish. Blueback led him past them to more drowned people. He saw little girls with lace dresses and drifting hair. He saw young men in seaboots with puffy white hands. And right at the end he found Mad Macka in his wetsuit beside the ragged body of Abel's father.

Blueback hovered over them. Abel looked down on his father, at the ragged hole in his side, at the grey skin of his cheeks. He was a young man still. No matter how old Abel grew, his father would always be thirty-two. His eyelids were pearly. He looked peaceful, asleep. Abel reached down to touch. He wanted to take his father back with him but Blueback finned upwards, keeping him out of reach. Abel lunged but the fish drew away and the boy saw his father's body grow small as they swam up through plankton and currents to the warmer, safer water of the surface.

Abel woke from that dream crying. The dormitory was dim. There was no one he could go to, no one to tell.

His mother wrote him letters and sent coral and shells. She mailed him a dried seahorse and a starfish. Now and then Abel picked up a turban shell from his bedside locker and held it to his ear. He knew it wasn't really the sea he heard, but he listened and let himself believe. He closed his eyes to school and the smell of dirty socks and the sight of the wide, flat land outside his window, and saw the ocean.

Chapter Six

Before the summer holidays Abel's mother wrote to tell him that a new abalone diver would be working their part of the coast this season. She was worried because she'd heard bad things about him. People said he was a reef stripper. But she had good news as well. Mad Macka's family had decided to give his boat to Abel. Boat, trailer, the lot. All his. Abel counted the days.

*

On the first day of the summer holidays, Abel's mother met the bus out on the highway. He saw her waiting in the truck on the gravel and he ran to her with his bags flying.

The moment he saw the green sea again his skin prickled. As they came out of the forest and onto Jackson land he hooted and crowed. The pair of them laughed all the way to the house. That night he stood on the jetty and breathed the salt air.

Next morning they dived for abalone off Robbers Head and Blueback flitted around them, insistent as a dog at the dinner table. Abel chucked him under the chin and felt the current the old fish made in the water.

That afternoon Abel stood on the beach beside Macka's big abalone boat. It was a five-metre catamaran, wide and stable as a house.

'I did some work on the motors,' said his mother. 'Four-stroke fifties. They're good outboards.'

Abel climbed up and stood on the deck. He tried not to think about the last time he was in this boat. The dive flag hung limp.

'You can clean it up yourself,' said his mother. 'We'll take the compressor off it today. We won't be needing the hookah.'

'What a boat,' said Abel.

'Let's get to work, then. Empty that icebox.'

✻

Abel took it slowly with the boat. His mother showed him how to handle it, how to use the echo sounder and the radios. He learnt how to trim the outboards in different sea conditions. For a few days they stayed in the bay. Then they moved out to Robbers Head and finally they took it out onto the dark, open sea. Abel steered them out across the sloping backs of oceanic swells as the land shrank to a long smudge behind them.

All afternoon they drifted for snapper, trailing heavy handlines with baits of squid. The snapper and morwong came up, flashing from the deep. Abel laid them in ice and felt the wind in his hair.

About three o'clock a huge, terrifying snort went up beside their boat. Then another across the bow and two more off the stern.

A foul mist rose over them and Abel saw the glistening backs of right whales all around.

'Look at that,' said his mother. 'We used to hunt them. Your father's family, the Jacksons, came here as whalers. Used to sit up on the ridge in a lookout and when they saw a pod of whales come by they'd row out in longboats and harpoon them.'

'I wonder if they remember, the whales.'

'Who knows. I hope not.'

Abel and his mother stopped fishing and just watched the whales.

'I used to feel bad about it,' said his mother, 'even though it was before our time. But the sea has taken its fair share of us. I think we must be even by now.'

Abel thought of all the crosses up behind the orchard.

A whale cruised past with its mouth wide.

It strained water through its baleen, rolling as it fed.

Abel laughed. 'Glad I'm not plankton, that's all I can say.'

Chapter Seven

That summer, as his skill and confidence grew, Abel took his boat up and down the coast exploring the long lonely stretches that made him feel small. Land and sea were so big he became dizzy just imagining how far they went. He felt like a speck, like a bubble on the sea left by a breaking wave, here for a moment and then gone. He pulled into tiny sheltered coves and swam with his mother in turquoise water beneath streaky cliffs and trees loud with birds. Some days he sped close in to long sugary beaches. He stayed just behind the breakers and was showered with their spray and saw the great, strange land through the wobbly glass of the waves. He saw the sun melting like butter on white dunes. Dolphins rose in his bow wave and he slapped them playfully with his rolled-up towel. He drifted amidst huge schools of tuna as they rose around him, feeding like packs of wild dogs on terrified baitfish that leapt across his boat.

Some days out east, he saw a big red jet-boat working its way along the coast with its dive flags streaming.

'Costello,' said his mother. 'The abalone diver. He's a hardcase.'

'He'll be here soon,' said Abel.

'I know,' said his mother.

'What about Blueback?'

'It's not just Blueback I'm worried about,' said his mother. 'It's the whole bay. People say he takes everything he sees.'

'So what do we do?'

'Nothing. We stay out of his way.'

'But Mum, what about Blueback?'

'He'll have to look after himself.'

'Can't we keep this bloke out of the bay?'

'This patch of land's ours, Abel. But the water belongs to everybody. Costello has a licence to take abalone. There's nothing we can do about it.'

'Can't someone stop him?'

'Only the Fisheries Department. They've been watching him.'

'But out here he can get away with anything, Mum. This is the middle of nowhere.'

Abel looked out across the moving water. He knew that when the time came he wouldn't just do nothing. He couldn't do nothing.

*

Abel swam with Blueback every chance he had. He tempted him with squid and cray legs. He felt the broad blade of the fish's tail against his chest and touched those flat white teeth with his fingertips. Abel held his breath and stared into the groper's face, trying to read it. Blueback swam down to his crack in the reef and looked out with moon eyes.

*

It was dawn when Abel heard the jet motor burbling into Longboat Bay. He climbed out of bed and found his way to the verandah. His mother was already there. The red boat slid in around the point and drifted with its motor off. An anchor splashed in the quiet. Then the compressor started up and two divers went over the side.

Abel's mother watched through binoculars.

'Things aren't the same, Abel. It's getting harder to hold on to good things.'

'Let's go out and cut his hoses,' said Abel.

'Don't talk like that.'

'Well, we have to stop him somehow.'

'We don't know that he's doing anything wrong.'

'And what happens when he starts doing wrong?'

She sighed. They went indoors.

At breakfast Abel's mother looked sad and thoughtful. All these holidays he'd been feeling bigger and older. Now that he looked properly he saw that his mother was ageing too. It was a surprise. To him she had always seemed the same age. In a year or so he'd be as tall as her.

'I've been wondering,' she said. 'Do you think I should sell up?'

Abel was speechless.

'I mean, I could buy a house inland,' she said. 'We could be together more.'

'But, Mum.'

'I suppose you're used to the hostel now. Living with your mother wouldn't be the same.'

'I hate the hostel,' said Abel. 'But you can't leave here.'

'But what if it's the best thing?'

'For who?'

'For you, Abel. Wouldn't you like more money? If I sold this place you'd have more chance to have things. We wouldn't have to work so hard fishing, planting, mending. Aren't you tired of being hard-up for money?'

'Mum, I don't care about money. And I love the fishing and growing stuff. This is what I want, the house, the land, the water. This is my life. I never want to leave.'

'But you'll have to leave sooner or later. There's a whole world out there. Believe me, Abel. You'll leave.'

'But not for good. And what about you? What would you be like away from the sea, Mum?'

She pushed her egg around the plate and chewed her lip. 'I'd be okay.'

'Tell the truth.'

'Abel, I always tell the truth.'

'Mum.'

'Oh, all right then, I hate it inland. I can't

bear the towns and cities. Of course I want to be here. I'm close to everything in Longboat Bay. All our memories. Your father. This is my place.'

Abel poured the tea. 'Are you lonely here on your own?'

'I miss you,' she murmured. 'I miss you terribly. But no, I'm not lonely. Sometimes I feel I should be. But this place is a kind of friend to me. Maybe I'm a bit odd.'

Abel thought about that. It was true, she wasn't like other people. She certainly wasn't like his schoolmates' mothers. Other mothers bought fashionable clothes and drove flash cars and chirped like birds. Abel's mother was quiet and tough and sun-streaked. She did things differently. Her hands were lined and calloused. She looked like the land and sea had made her.

'I want to stay here, Abel. I want to die here.'

'Mum, you're not that old. Don't talk like that.'

'Like what? I don't intend to die tomorrow. I plan to kick the bucket as a very old lady. But I want to do it here, not in some awful town away from the sea.'

Abel laughed. 'Well, that's okay then.'

He got up and went to the window. The jetboat had worked along the bay a few hundred metres. Abel picked up the binoculars and saw a diver hoisting up a huge bag of abalone. Another bag came up. Then a string of bleeding fish wired to a red buoy. Abel began to sweat.

'Costello's giving the bay a real hammering,' he said. 'He'll be at Robbers Head by lunchtime the way he's going. There won't be anything left on the reef at all. It's wrong, Mum.'

His mother said nothing.

'Mum?' he pleaded.

'Costello's a hardcase, Abel. He's a vicious man. You're thirteen years old.'

Abel put the binoculars down and kicked the wall.

After breakfast they pulled weeds in the vegetable garden. It was boring work in the hard sun. The soil was full of tiny bones that cut their fingertips. Abel saw that his hands had gone soft at school. His mother hummed a tune. As the morning wore on he grew more agitated. He kept an eye on the bay, saw bag after bag of abalone hauled up and it was like being pricked by fishbones all over.

'Mum,' he said. 'I can't stand it.'

'We don't have any choice.'

'Well, I'm making my choice.'

He ran downhill to the house and grabbed his wetsuit off the verandah rail.

'Abel, don't!'

He stumped along the jetty. As he leapt into his boat he heard his mother thudding along the timbers. He checked his fuel and started his outboards. His mother's wetsuit dropped onto the deck. He looked up. She was casting off the lines.

'This is stupid and dangerous,' she said.

'So why come?'

'Because if you went on your own it would be twice as stupid and twice as dangerous.'

Abel throttled up and they swerved out, thumping across the bay with the wind streaming in their hair.

*

When they got to the anchored boat at Robbers Head Abel eased the boat down to dead slow then cut his motors so they could drift up alongside. Costello's compressor roared and his flags snapped in the breeze.

The deck of Costello's boat was awash with blood. Abel had speared fish nearly every day but he had never seen such slaughter as this. Fish lay in huge slippery mounds and so many of them were undersize. Abel saw blue morwong, trevally, sweep, boarfish, harlequins, breaksea cod, groper, jewfish and samsons stiffening in the sun or quivering slowly to death. Behind the steering console stood crates of writhing abalone and a box of illegal crayfish.

'We should chuck the abs back over the side,' Abel said. 'They might survive.'

'You step on that boat, son, and you'll get horribly hurt. I won't have it.'

Abel sighed and pushed his boat clear. They drifted back in the breeze away from the dive zone.

'Now what?' asked Abel.

Abel's mother was snapping on a weight-belt and wetting her mask.

'I want you to stay with the boat, you understand? It's important.'

'But Mum!'

She went over the side before he could argue any further. He watched her fins flash away into the distance. Abel had no intention of staying dry. He anchored the boat, pulled on his gear and rolled out into the clear, cool water.

He swam across to the red boat, climbed up the ladder and began emptying crates of abalone over the side. Then he dived back in and followed the bright, trailing hoses down to the blossom of bubbles that marked where the divers worked. Once he found them he swam back to the surface and watched from there. In a scattered mass behind them, falling like snow, abalone were finding their way back onto the reef. Some were dead and knots of little fish picked at them. But the divers didn't look back. They lay on the rugged bottom with spearguns.

One diver pointed something out to the other. Bubbles smoked back from his head so that he looked like a dragon. There was a blue flash ahead of them. Abel's heart sank. He knew exactly what it would be. He took a breath and dived.

He was only halfway to the bottom when he saw Blueback dart out from behind a boulder. He was as big as a barrel; he made a big target. A spear flashed silver. It flew by Blueback's head and whanged into hard rock. The fish shuddered for a moment, staring at the divers and then retreated a little way.

Abel knew why. It was all the abalone he'd tipped into the water. Blueback was wary but he couldn't resist all that food. Behind the divers, swarms of smaller fish were feasting and Blueback wanted to be in on it. Only the two men lay in his way. He flicked back and forward, excited, blinded by his appetite.

Abel ran out of air. He shot back to the surface. Blueback was doomed now, he knew it. In a moment or two a spear would hit him in the gills and the water would go pink with his blood.

Then suddenly Abel's mother appeared between the divers and the fish. She surged out from behind a rock and put her body in the way. Blueback swirled around her play-fully. No, Abel thought, you stupid fish. Don't be friendly! Hole up, rack off, go away!

One diver reloaded. Then the both of them crept forward, billowing bubbles. Their spearguns glinted like shiny stings. Abel could see his mother was short of breath now. Her strength was going. The fish kept circling her, exposing its side to the spearguns. Abel began to panic. His mother would drown down there. The fish would die. These men would beat him to mush.

Then, in a blur, the fish was gone and Abel's mother came pumping and kicking hard for the surface. He swam over to where she punched up into the air. He dragged her mask off and let her heave and blow. She felt limp in his arms as he swam her to the boat.

'Stupid fish,' she wheezed, hanging weakly off the ladder.

'What happened?'

'I told you to stay out of the water. And what about that idiotic business with the abalone? Abel, you—'

'Mum, what *happened*? He was fooling around and then – whoosh – he was off.'

'He wanted to play. I didn't have any air left. Those fellas were determined to get him.'

'So he got smart, eh?'

'Not likely.'

'Well?'

'I biffed him one. I punched him in the head.'

'Costello?'

'No, Abel. The *fish*. I thumped him one. To scare him off.'

Abel laughed. 'Man alive! And it worked.'

'Took off like a rocket. He won't like me anymore, that's for sure. Probably got a black eye.'

'Well, it's better than ending up as fish fingers.'

'Let's go, Abel. Those blokes will be a little hot under the collar. They'll need to decompress a while before they come up, so let's be off while we can.'

'Will there be trouble?'

'Probably. We've done it now.'

Abel helped her aboard and took her home. It was true, she wasn't your average mother. Abel decided he didn't care about average. Out here average didn't seem worth bothering with.

Chapter Eight

Abel and his mother went ashore to wait for trouble. But trouble never came. Once or twice they saw the mirror flash of binoculars upon them, but fairly soon the compressor started up again and Costello and his offsider went back to stripping the reef bare, as though nothing could keep them from business. Plenty of abalone came to the surface but no speared fish, and, to Abel's great relief, no huge blue groper. Old Blueback stayed holed up, nursing his sore head, safe from spears.

Then, quite abruptly, at four o'clock, a Fisheries patrol boat swung in around the headland and skated across Longboat Bay. It ran alongside Costello's boat and three officers boarded her. Half an hour later the abalone boat left Robbers Head at the end of a tow rope with a cloud of gulls off her stern. As it steamed out onto the open sea, the patrol boat let off a blast of its horn that echoed all the way into the forest.

*

For the rest of that summer, Blueback kept clear of Abel's mother. Costello's fines cost him his licence and put him out of business. Abel was a little disappointed that he had never met the man. It would have been thrilling to come face to face with a real-life villain.

But a couple of weeks after the Costello business, Abel got to know enough about the man to know he never wanted to meet him after all.

A huge tiger shark swam into the bay. Abel took his boat out to see the thing swimming sluggishly up and down the beach. His mother stayed ashore; she said she never wanted to see a tiger shark again as long as she lived. Abel couldn't blame her but his curiosity got the better of him.

The shark looked wrinkled and flabby when it should have been thick and powerful as a tree. It wasn't hard to see why. Everywhere it went it towed a big red buoy on a length of chain. It had a stainless steel meathook in its jaws and it swam like a ghost of itself. The shark couldn't dive without being defeated by the buoy and dragged painfully back to the surface. The day it was hooked it would have dragged it underwater for hours but now its strength was gone and every turn of its head, every kick of the tail was agony. The buoy dragged behind like a ball on a chain. The tiger shark was starving to death and dying of exhaustion. It was a pitiful sight and it sickened Abel. If he'd had a gun he would have pulled alongside and shot it through the head to end its suffering. There was no way he could save the shark now, even if he could cut it free.

So Abel watched the shark all afternoon. In the end he came ashore and watched it from the jetty. It swam feebly up and down, restless with its terrible agony. That night he sat on the verandah and saw moonlight flash on the dragging buoy which made a miserable sparkling wake on the still water.

In the morning the tiger shark was dead. The tide left it stiff and leathery on the beach and Abel turned the red buoy over in his hands to see the name stencilled on the side. COSTELLO.

He towed the shark out to sea, replaced the buoy with some lead weights and cut it free. It sailed down into the black deep like a torpedoed ship.

Abel went back to school in the new year feeling older, different. That summer he learnt that there was nothing in nature as cruel and savage as a greedy human being.

Chapter Nine

In his high school years, Abel Jackson felt like he was holding his breath. It was like diving, only not nearly as much fun. From the moment he left Longboat Bay at the beginning of every semester, something inside him took a deep breath and held on until he got back. Like a good diver he taught himself to relax, to resist panic, to believe he had the strength to do what he needed to do.

During those years he wondered if his mother would marry again. It didn't seem right that she should live out on the coast alone. She was still beautiful and strong. Men liked her and looked up to her but she seemed to fend them off like friendly puppies. Secretly, Abel knew that he wouldn't like to go home to find someone else, a strange man, in his life. Still, he did want her to be happy. But Dora Jackson, his mother, never married again.

It was during these years that the developers came to Longboat Bay. They were businessmen and councillors in suits and BMWs who wanted to build a resort in the bay. All the land around the Jackson place was national park and could never be touched. But a hotel and golf course and swimming pool and a marina could all fit on Jackson land. When these men saw Longboat Bay they saw money, piles of it. Rich tourists, they thought, could moor their yachts and sit out on resort balconies here and watch kangaroos grazing at the edge of the forest. International entrepreneurs could play golf and make deals. Helicopters could bring people in daily for whalewatching tours. Charter boats could take fishermen out every morning. And scuba lovers could meet that big old groper the Jackson kid played with every day. To them it was a goldmine, a fortune waiting to be made.

But Dora Jackson didn't want to sell. The businessmen were friendly at first. Their fat red faces were splitting with grins. They brought flowers and chocolates and bottles of champagne. Little gifts were followed by bigger gifts: a new outboard motor, a wind generator. This is no place for a woman on her own, they said. They offered her good money, but she didn't sell. They brought experts, tax men, lawyers, agents, but still she told them politely that she didn't want to sell. The smiles faded. The gifts stopped coming.

And then little things, annoying things, began to happen. The Longboat Bay road began to get rougher and more potholed because the council grader never seemed to come. The mail was always late or wet or it never came at all. Deliveries of diesel fuel and petrol had water in them so that Dora Jackson's outboards and generators and truck engine began to stall. There were mysterious bushfires in the forest in the middle of winter.

Abel read about it in his mother's letters,

angry that he could not be there to help out. At night he lay awake thinking of her and the bay. He knew she would hold out against whatever the money men did. She was stubborn as a tree and just as strong. But he hated how it wore her down, wasted her time, pinched at her nerves. Those men didn't understand that a place isn't just a property. They didn't see that Longboat Bay was a life to his mother, a friend. And maybe a husband to her as well.

Every day at that peppermint tree there she was, thinking about Abel's father. It puzzled him how a person could do that year after year. But as he grew older, Abel could see how strong her love was for all these things: the sea, the bush, the house, her husband's memory. It was love that stopped her from being lonely, that made her strong.

It was like food to her. Abel knew that it was his mother's love that kept him going all those dull high school years while he was stuck inland, holding his breath until he was blue in the face.

Abel Jackson's mother beat the sneaky businessmen. She simply outlasted them. Her calm patience wore them out. They got bored and fed up, and after five years they left her alone.

Chapter Ten

Abel had graduated from high school and was home on the holidays when all the pilchards died. There was no storm, no warning, no oil spill, no explanation. One morning he stumped down to the jetty to see the whole beach blackened with dead fish. The air roared with flies. Gulls hovered uncertainly over the stinking mess. Abel walked along the beach trying to understand it. He helped his mother load the truck with mushy piles of the fish and for hours they spread them on the soil of the orchard and the gardens.

'Something's wrong with the sea,' said his mother. 'This isn't right. It's not normal.'

Late that day, Abel took his boat out and dived in the bay, along the point and out at Robbers Head. The abalone had recovered from the season that Costello had come. Trevally and tarwhine and garfish twitched along in healthy schools. Everything looked normal. The kelp and the coral were alive. He fooled around with Blueback and biffed him a couple of times with his hip as he passed close by. All of it seemed ordinary, usual.

He thought about Blueback that evening. If only fish could talk. Maybe then Blueback could tell him how the water felt, whether something was wrong somewhere along the coast or in the deeps.

Abel sat on the verandah with his feet on the rail, thinking about it. Imagine that, he thought, knowing what the old fish knew. Blueback was probably old enough to have known Abel's mother as a girl. Hadn't she come out here as a teenager, staying summers with his father's family? Did he see them swimming together, his parents? Two young lovers. Had his father dived down to look at a small greenish groper out at Robbers Head one day? People said his father swam like a fish. They said sometimes he thought he was a fish. If Blueback could speak, thought Abel, he could tell him about his father. All the secrets of the sea would be there waiting for him.

When Abel went inside that night his

mother caught him staring at the photo on the mantelpiece.

'You look like him, you know.'

Abel shook his head. But then he looked again and saw that it was true. He had his father's face.

*

Later that month, tuna skippers told the Jacksons that pilchards were floating dead all along the coast. No one had a clue what it was about.

'The ocean is sick,' said Abel's mother. 'Something's wrong.'

It was a mystery. And the more he thought about it the more the whole sea seemed to be a puzzle. Abel wanted to figure it out.

Chapter Eleven

Abel Jackson went to university to figure out the sea. His mother smiled about that. He'd lived half his life underwater, his best friend was a fish and now he was leaving Longboat Bay to learn about the sea. It seemed a bit mad to her but she shrugged her shoulders and let him go.

Abel moved to the city. The university

was like a small town inside the city itself. It was ugly and dreary and full of talk. In his university years, Abel pretended to be a scientist. He explored the sea with computer modelling, with books and specimens in jars, with photos and films. Now and then he went on field trips with other students. He dived in new places, from new islands and boats and beaches, but he felt the same old sea on his body, through his hair, in his ears.

Between semesters he came home and sat on the verandah at Longboat Bay and knew he was no closer to knowing what fish think. He saw whales spouting and dolphins surfing. With his mother he netted salmon and smoked herring. He painted the house and patched the driveway. In autumn he scraped out the watertanks and pruned the vines. One year he brought home some solar panels so they didn't need the noisy generator anymore. That was the year he fell in love.

Abel Jackson met a girl who loved the sea. She was sleek as a seal and funny. Her hair was black and shiny. She grew up in the desert and didn't see the ocean until she was twelve years old. Her name was Stella. That summer Abel brought Stella to Longboat Bay.

When he climbed out of his car and introduced Stella to his mother, Abel was surprised at how lined his mother's face was. With a young woman standing beside her, Dora Jackson looked old. There were lines like gulls' feet all over her face. To him she'd always been young, but now, standing beside Stella, her skin seemed dry and papery.

She was an old woman. I'm away too much, he thought. I'm missing things.

Abel was nervous that first day, worried that the two women would not like each other. He saw that his mother knew it. Her smile said it all.

'Stella,' she said, 'you know that you'll have to share Abel, don't you?'

'Of course,' said Stella. 'You're his mother.'

Dora Jackson laughed. 'Actually, I was thinking of somebody else. Abel, let's show her who we mean.'

So the three of them went out to Robbers Head and swam with Blueback. The old groper flirted with them and ate crabs out of their hands. Stella shrieked in her snorkel when he nuzzled up to her. The fish's eyes twitched and his gills heaved. He looked as fat as an opera singer.

When they swam back to the boat Abel saw that his mother had trouble climbing the ladder to get aboard. He floated up behind and boosted her up. She laughed, suddenly embarrassed. Blueback swirled deep below them, just a blur.

That evening they had a feast on the cool verandah. The table bristled with crayfish and abalone. They ate squid and urchin eggs, apricots, grapes and melons. Cold champagne frosted their glasses and sweated on the driftwood table. Stella watched Abel and his mother.

'You two,' she said. 'You seem to be able to talk to each other without saying anything.'

'Practice,' said Abel.

'It's the fish in us,' said Dora Jackson. 'We don't always need words.'

Out on the moonlit bay, dolphins jumped

and hooted. It was like a celebration. Abel remembered the dolphins as a good omen because that was the night he asked Stella to marry him.

Chapter Twelve

Abel Jackson became a marine biologist married to another marine biologist. With Stella he travelled and studied, diving in all the oceans and seas of the world. In time he became an expert, someone foreign governments invited for lectures and study tours, but inside he still felt like a boy with a snorkel staring at the strange world underwater, wishing he knew how it worked. Blueback still swam through his dreams.

He was diving in the Greek islands one day, looking at the great underwater desert that dynamite fishing and pollution had created, when he realised that he was older than his father. It came as a cold shock. His father would always be a young man; he never grew older than the moment that tiger shark loomed out of the murk and broke him in two.

That very day he got back to his hotel and found a diving magazine on his bed. On the front cover Blueback and two divers circled each other like dancers.

There was a letter from his mother.

Lots of people came this year, Abel. Boat after boat full of divers wanting to swim with that fat old fish.

Some days I have fifteen boats in the bay.
Not all of them are welcome, I must say.
People come spearing in groups. I'm worried
about the bay.

A month later an oil tanker cracked in two off the coast of Longboat Bay. Abel watched it on TV from halfway across the world. In another city, and another hotel room, he saw video pictures of the oil slick spreading. In an airport lounge next day he passed a TV and watched the same ship catch fire and the slick burn up as foul weather drove the mess away and broke it up. The stricken ship drifted far out to sea until the weather improved enough for it to be towed back to port. No oil ever reached the shore. Abel Jackson knew how close the whole coast had come to disaster. He called his mother and let her know that he had seen the drama. She cried when she heard his voice. It's a warning, she told him.

As he travelled with Stella, going where their work took them, to coral atolls, to estuaries choking on pollutants, to strange countries and new oceans, Abel thought about his home all year long and felt the big blue fish pressing against him in his sleep.

Chapter Thirteen

Dora Jackson had been worrying for years when the storm came. Each year the weather grew more fierce and erratic. Strange things happened every season. One year a leopard seal arrived on the beach all the way from Antarctica. Another year the salmon didn't show at all. She found five dead dolphins snagged in the cliffs at Robbers Head. Abel and Stella wrote letters and called but they were too busy with work to come home much anymore and Dora had trouble keeping everything going on her own now. The orchard was getting away from her. Rabbits got into the vegetables at night and foxes to the hens. Her fingers were stiff with arthritis and engines defeated her.

She took Abel's old boat out some days to fish or she walked with her thoughts along the beach and through the karri trees. In winter the bay was quiet, the way it used to be. No boats came. The place could be itself.

When it came, the storm was like a cyclone. It blew down her fences and took the roof off her freezer shed. The sea grew tormented. It buckled and swelled and bunted against the cliffs and headlands. Surf hammered the shore and chewed it away. The air was thick with foam and sand and spray. Wind gusts screamed till she covered her ears. The old house rattled and rocked like an old lugger at sea. Dora Jackson lay in bed until it was all over.

Late in the morning she got up to see the mess. She walked down to the shore to see a strange jumble of white stumps on the beach. As she got close she saw they were whale bones, thousands and thousands of them all along the bay. They stood like posts and broken teeth and tombstones where the storm had exposed them. Dora Jackson stepped over and under and around them. It was like walking through a graveyard. These bones had lain here under the sand of Longboat Bay for a century or more. She'd walked over them for forty years without knowing. It was a terrible feeling having history unearth itself so suddenly.

She sat all day with bones around her, bones the Jacksons had left here in their whaling days. It was whaling and sealing that brought the Jacksons here in wooden ships last century. Blubber oil and baleen, seal fur and fish had paid for this land over time. The Jacksons were all dead now, generations of men, women and children, and only Abel and her were left. It had come down to them. They had lived from the sea all this time. Dora saw what must be done. Now it was time to help the sea live. She must protect the bay for all time.

That night in the wreckage of her house, Dora Jackson began writing letters. She wrote till dawn and the next night she went at it again. She wrote hundreds of them. They were like a coral spawn, those letters, tiny white messages that drifted out from Longboat Bay into the offices of people all over the country. Politicians, bosses, scientists all ignored her, but they had no idea how stubborn she could be. Month after month the letters went out, over and over, back and forward. Photos of Blueback landed on the desks of newspaper editors. There was something about that fat blue face with its moony eye which seemed to look right into you. Abel's mother was patient. She outlasted them all.

*

Abel and Stella were diving in the warm everclear water of a rare lagoon when the fax came through on the expedition boat. Abel read it before he had towelled himself dry. He read it aloud to Stella as she peeled out of her suit. The message said that Longboat Bay had been declared a sanctuary, a marine park where everything that grew and swam there was protected by law. Stella went straight up the companionway to the bridge and called in a chopper. Abel went below to pack.

*

On the plane home, high over the Pacific Ocean, Abel Jackson had a dream. In the dream his mother was dead. She floated in Longboat Bay like seaweed as he swam from shore to reach her. Gulls and terns whirled above her, wailing. As he reached her he touched her face, her old, beautiful face, and she sank beneath the surface. She tilted over and wheeled like a starfish into the blackest deep. Out of the blur came a dark shape.

Blueback. The old fish followed her down into the darkness, his tail swinging like a gate as they both disappeared.

'You're crying,' said Stella when he woke.

'Yes.'

'Was it a bad dream?'

'No, not bad. Sad, I suppose. All these years I just wanted to know about the sea. I've been everywhere, I've studied, I've given lectures, become a bigshot. But you know, my mother is still the one who understands it. She doesn't go anywhere at all. She grows vegetables and eats fish. And she's saved a place. I'm a scientist, a big cheese, but I've never saved a place. She learnt by staying put, by watching and listening. Feeling things. She didn't need a computer and two degrees and a frequent flyer program. She's part of the bay. That's how she knows it.'

The jet rumbled beneath them. Stella squeezed his hand.

'But you had to leave, Abel. You had school and work to think of.'

He shrugged. 'But all I ever wanted to do was figure out what keeps it all together. When I was a boy I just wanted to know what Blueback thought about things. I wanted to learn the language of the sea.'

'Like Dora says, maybe you don't need words.'

The plane rumbled on, taking him home.

Chapter Fourteen

The night Abel returned, there was a little party on the verandah at Longboat Bay. The sea murmured against the shore and humpbacks sang somewhere out in the dark beyond Robbers Head. It was a hot, still night and the salt air hung upon them. Dora Jackson told them stories of waterspouts and lightning balls and manta rays and schools of salmon so thick you could climb out of your boat and walk across them. All the wonders of the ocean, the things she'd seen. She held the papers from the government that protected the bay as a sanctuary. The pages flashed yellow in the light of the lantern. Her face glowed with pride and relief. The three of them laughed and sang until it was late, celebrating the news, happy to be together again.

They were all going to bed when Abel's mother fell. She stumbled against the rail and toppled down the verandah steps to the hard dirt below. She cried out, her voice small as a girl's.

Abel rushed to her and saw that her hip was broken. Stella called an ambulance and they wrapped her in blankets for the long wait.

'I'm old, Abel,' she sobbed. 'I'm sorry, but I'm old.'

He held her and cried with her under the warm, starry sky. She was too old to stay on here alone. Sooner or later she would have to leave and that was why she was crying. It hurt her more than the pain itself and Abel understood why.

✳

During the long weeks his mother was in hospital, Abel began to clean the old Jackson place up. He was appalled and ashamed at how run-down the house and gardens had become. The jetty timbers were rotting. Fences and sheds were falling over and the orchard had begun to go wild.

The telephone rang day and night with calls from cities and beaches all over the world. A crisis here, some emergency there, but Abel kept at the job of fixing his family place.

One afternoon he walked up past the orchard to the peppermint tree and stood there a long time. He thought about his father and felt close to his memory there. He put his cheek against the rough bark the way he had as a boy and hugged the thick trunk.

At sunset he stood on the jetty and watched a big blue shadow circle beneath him and peel off into the golden light. The wind luffed at his hair. Cicadas in the dry grass clicked their tongues. Crabs bubbled and clattered across the rocks. Whalebones made a chain all the way along the beach, yellow in the sunset. Abel felt the place was calling him; it made him dizzy.

His wife joined him on the jetty.

'How will she live somewhere else?' he asked her. 'My mother'll die in a town.'

'I know,' said Stella. 'She should stay here.'

'She can't do it alone.'

'That's why we're staying,' said Stella.

Abel laughed. 'Really?'

'Abel, do you want to talk about the sea or be in it?'

He shuffled his feet.

'Do you want to be homesick or be home?'

He looked out at the water, purpling towards night. 'It's a hard life here, Stella.'

'So why do you lie awake every night wishing you were here?'

'Because it's what I want,' he said. 'It's what I always wanted.'

'I rang the Foundation a few minutes ago and told them we quit.'

✳

Abel brought his mother home to a freshly painted house. She was surprised at the yards and the fixed sheds and newly planted gardens. They made a special bed on the shady verandah and nursed her back to health. Dora stood with the aid of a walking frame the day the officials came to declare the bay a marine reserve. She pointed out the politicians who used to be business-men, the same ones who wanted to build hotels here. With great satisfaction she watched them set the marker buoys that showed the boundaries of the sanctuary. It stretched all the way out to Robbers Head, a safe place at last. She wanted more of them, other havens along the coast, but for now she was content.

In time Abel's mother was walking again, but she never went far without help. Some days she took a chair down to the jetty. When she was strong she made the climb up to the peppermint tree to be alone with her memories.

The three of them mended nets and bottled fruit and smoked fish and told long, ludicrous stories as they worked. Abel and Stella supervised the bay and kept an eye on the summer visitors. They wrote papers on the breeding habits of abalone. They walked in the forest and sat up high on the ridge to watch the migrating whales pass. Some days they took divers to see Blueback gobble crabs and swim grumpily round his reef.

*

One cold winter night a baby was born at Longboat Bay. They called her Dora after her grandmother. Her fists were like pink sea shells and she cried like a bird.

Chapter Fifteen

After a few years Abel's mother could no longer walk along the beach she loved. She was too frail to dive anymore and too stiff to pick fruit or dig vegetables. In the end she lay in her bed and listened to the sea. On fine days Abel carried her to the verandah so she could watch the tide and see the life of the ocean. Her hair was white as the sand on the shore and little Dora liked to feel it silky between her fingers. Old Dora Jackson slept a lot but when she woke she told stories.

'When Abel was born,' she said, 'his father thought we should let him meet the sea straight away so he wouldn't get homesick. After all, he'd been swimming inside me all that time. He was always a swimmer. So we took him down while the water was warm. We knelt in the shallows and lowered him gently into the sea. For a moment he went stiff as coral and then he kicked like a fish about to be set free. He wanted to swim off right there and then. He cried when I took him back to the house. He was always like that. Just like his father. Couldn't get him out of the water.'

✳

The day before Dora Jackson died, Abel carried her gingerly down from the verandah and took her to the shore. Her nightie flapped and her hair became a tumbleweed in the breeze. He walked out a little way as whiting darted past his feet. He cradled her in his arms, laid her back and let her float against him in the clear, still water.

'We come from water,' she whispered. 'We belong to it, Abel.'

She lay back smiling, her arms and legs bobbing lightly. She weighed nothing at all. A long, blue shadow swerved into the shallows and swam around them once, stirring up the sand like confetti against them.

The next afternoon she died in her sleep and Abel made a new cross for the little graveyard behind the orchard.

Chapter Sixteen

Abel Jackson never regretted staying on at Longboat Bay. He lived the life of his boyhood every day and he was happy. The bay grew rich with life as fish came into it for sanctuary. They seemed to know that, just past Robbers Head, hooks and nets awaited them. They bred in their haven and swelled the stocks of the coast beyond.

Seagrass, coral and sponges thrived. Abalone grew like snails in a garden. Dolphins and sharks came in. Sea lions returned to Robbers Head after being gone a hundred years. People dived into this teeming world and saw how the ocean could be itself.

Abel and Stella went back to being scientists. People came to visit them from all over the world and they continued to watch and listen and read. But they never discovered the secret of the sea. Abel figured his mother knew all the secrets by now and his father before her. He guessed that Mad Macka might have a few ideas too and that his own time would come eventually. In the meantime he let the sea be itself.

✲

On little Dora Jackson's third birthday, three divers drifted in clear water off Robbers Head. The smallest diver hung like a sail between the grownups as they flew down to the rubbly bottom.

Out of the shadows, from a crack in the reef, a huge blue creature came swirling at them. The little girl's eyes grew big in her mask and she chirped in her snorkel.

The fish's head was enormous. She felt that it was about to swallow her and she pressed against her parents in panic. But Blueback slipped in close to them, fins rippling. His scales shone. His tail fanned. He was the colour of all their dreams and he rested against the child, quivering with life.